LITTLE HOUSE

Laura Ingalls Wilder

MY FIRST LITTLE HOUSE BOOKS

THE DEER
IN THE
WOOD

ADAPTED FROM THE LITTLE HOUSE BOOKS

By Laura Ingalls Wilder

Illustrated by Renée Graef

SCHOLASTIC INC.
New York Toronto London Auckland Sydney

For Katie
—R.G.

ISBN 0-590-92892-9

Text adapted from *Little House In the Big Woods*, copyright © 1932, copyright renewed 1959 by Roger Lea MacBride. Illustrations copyright © 1995 by Renée Graef.

All rights reserved. Published by Scholastic Inc., 555 Broadway, New York, NY 10012, by arrangement with HarperCollins Publishers.

SCHOLASTIC and associated logos are trademarks and/or registered trademarks of Scholastic Inc.

12 11 10 9 8 7 6 5 4 3 2 1   7 8 9/9 0 1 2/0

Printed in the U.S.A.   14

First Scholastic printing, December 1997

"Little House" ® is a registered trademark of HarperCollins Publishers, Inc. U.S. Registration No. 1,771,442.

Illustrations for the My First Little House Books are inspired by the work of Garth Williams with his permission, which we gratefully acknowledge.

Once upon a time, a little girl named Laura lived in the Big Woods of Wisconsin in a little house made of logs.

Laura lived in the little house with her Pa, her Ma,
her big sister Mary, her baby sister Carrie, and
their good old bulldog Jack.

It was autumn, and the days were getting short
and cold. A fire burned all day in the cookstove to
keep the little house warm. Laura and Mary worked
on their patchwork quilts in front of the fire.

One night Pa said that after supper he would go into the Big Woods to look for a deer. There had been no meat in the little house since spring, and it was time for Pa to go hunting again.

After supper Pa went into the Big Woods. Laura and Mary went to bed, and they missed the songs Pa always played for them on his fiddle before they fell asleep.

The next day Laura and Mary waited for Pa to tell them about the deer. But Pa was busy all day chopping firewood so the little house would stay warm inside. And there was no deer meat for supper that night.

After supper Pa took Laura on his knee, while Mary sat close on her little chair. Pa said, "Now I'll tell you why we had no meat today.

"Last night I went into the woods and climbed up into a big oak tree to watch for a deer," Pa said. "Soon the big round moon rose, and I could see a deer with great big horns that stood out from his head.

"He looked so strong and free and wild that I couldn't shoot him. I sat and looked at him until he ran off into the Big Woods.

"Then I remembered that Ma and my girls were waiting for me to bring home some meat for supper. So I made up my mind that the next time I saw a deer, I would shoot.

"After a long while a mother deer and her baby fawn stepped into the moonlight. They stood there together, looking out into the woods. Their large eyes were shining and soft.

"I just sat there looking at them until they walked away among the shadows. Then I climbed down out of the tree and came home."

Laura whispered in his ear, "I'm glad you didn't shoot them!"

And Mary said, "We can eat bread and butter."

Pa hugged both of them together and said, "You're my good girls."

Soon Laura and Mary were tucked snugly under their covers, Pa played his fiddle softly, and Ma sat by the fireplace, gently rocking and knitting. And Laura lay awake a little while, thinking how lucky they were to be so safe and cozy in their little house in the Big Woods.